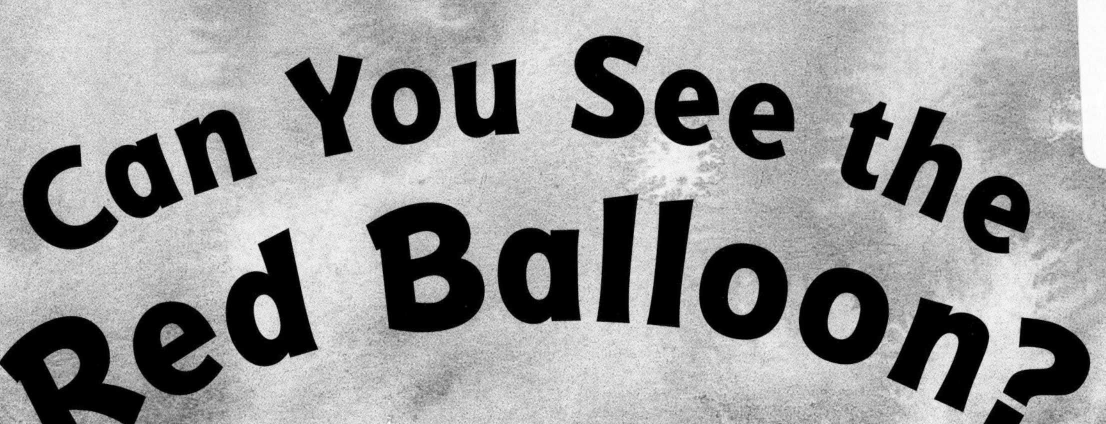

Can You See the Red Balloon?

Written by Stella Blackstone

Illustrated by Debbie Harter

Barefoot Books

Celebrating Art and Story

Can you see

the red dessert, the red dog, the red streamers, the red sun, the red balls, the red feathers,

the red balloon?
the red party hat, the red plate, the red spider, the red party blower, and Florence the black-and-white cow.

Can you see
the white bones, the white owl, the white ghosts, the white spider, the white lightning, the white astronaut,

the white moon?

the white teeth, the white spaceship, the white web, the white sheep, and Florence the black-and-white cow.

Can you see

the blue pond, the blue pillow, the blue birds, the blue gate, the blue bug, the blue caterpillar.

the blue flower?

the blue birdhouse, the blue butterflies, the blue tire, and Florence the black-and-white cow.

Can you see
the orange cat, the orange roofs, the orange boat, the orange sails, the orange flag, the orange fish.

the orange tower?

the orange Popsicle, the orange umbrella, the orange starfish, and Florence the black-and-white cow.

Can you see
the gray faucets, the gray pan, the gray spoon, the gray bottle top, the gray dog dish, the gray knife,

the gray mouse?

the gray stool, the gray knobs, the gray handles, and Florence the black-and-white cow.

Can you see

the purple donkeys, the purple baby carriage, the purple streetlamps, the purple flowers, the purple clock tower,

the purple house?

the purple curtains, the purple chimneys, the purple roofs, the purple doors, and Florence the black-and-white cow.

Can you see

the green plant, the green duck, the green dresser, the green basket, the green picture frame,

the green quilt, the green doorknobs, the green mouse, the green vase, and Florence the black-and-white cow.

the green sock?

Can you see
the black lamp, the black picture frame, the black mouse, the black spider, the black bee,

the black clock?

the black bird, the black tiles, the black doorknobs, and Florence the black-and-white cow.

Can you see

the pink pigs, the pink skateboard, the pink flowers, the pink tractor, the pink bicycle,

the pink car?

the pink fenders, the pink dashboard, the pink motorcycle, and Florence the black-and-white cow.

Can you see
the yellow camels, the yellow moons, the yellow fish, the yellow crowns, the yellow rabbit, the yellow presents,

the yellow star?

the yellow lights, the yellow bows, the yellow birds, and Florence the black-and-white cow.

Can you see
the colorful butterfly, the colorful bird, the colorful rainbow, the colorful horse, the colorful caterpillar.

the colorful barn, the colorful cat, the colorful sheep, the colorful chicken, and Florence the colorful cow.
colorful me?

Barefoot Books
2067 Massachusetts Avenue
Cambridge, MA 02140

First published in the United Kingdom in 1997 by Barefoot Books
This edition first published in paperback by Barefoot Books, Inc. in 2004

The illustrations were prepared in watercolor, crayon, pen and ink on thick watercolor paper

Graphic design by Tom Grzelinski, Bath
Color separation by Grafiscan, Verona
Printed in Singapore by Tien Wah Press Pte Ltd

This book has been printed on 100% acid-free paper

1 3 5 7 9 8 6 4 2

Library of Congress Cataloging-in-Publication Data

Blackstone, Stella.
Can you see the red balloon? / by Stella Blackstone ; illustrated by Debbie Harter. –
p. cm.
Summary: The reader is asked to pick out objects of different colors in each picture, plus the black-and-white cow that appears on every page.
ISBN 1-84148-788-0 (pbk.)
[1. Colors—Fiction.] I. Harter, Debbie, ill II. Title.
PZ7.B5333Can 1998 [E]—dc21 97-26673